Cowboy
Boy

Cowboy Boy

James Proimos

AN
APPLE
PAPERBACK

SCHOLASTIC INC.

New York Toronto London Auckland Sydney
Mexico City New Delhi Hong Kong Buenos Aires

ISBN 0-439-56032-2

12 11 10 9 8 7 6 5 4 3 2 1   3 4 5 6 7 8/0

Printed in the U.S.A.   40

First paperback printing, October 2003

The art in this book was created with a Sharpie on paper, scanned, and then colored on an iMac in Adobe Photoshop LE.

The text type was set in Fink Roman 13-point.

Original book design by Yvette Awad

Dedicated

to the

amazing Jimmy

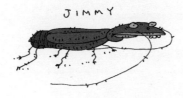

and the

stupendous Annie.

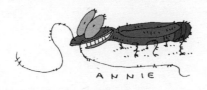

Inspired by

my hero,

Bernadine.

Introduction

What you're about to read is a fable, a parable,
   a tall tale, if you will.
The essence of everything is true.
I may have exaggerated here and there. . . .
Perhaps my parents aren't all that massively awful.
Maybe my best friend doesn't go on quite so much.
Maybe my teachers weren't exactly quoted verbatim.
Maybe my transformation wasn't quite so dramatic.
Know this: All the supersizing I've done is to make you
   understand the whole truth more truly.
The truth about how parents can get under your skin.
The truth about bullies and what makes them tick.
The truth about being afraid in a great big world.
And the crazy things that can give you the confidence
   to see life in an entirely new way.

RICKY SMOOTZ

My name is Ricky V. Smootz.
The V stands for Very Afraid.
That's right, my middle name is Very Afraid.
Well, that's not what's on my birth certificate.
But it may as well be.
Or have been.

I was afraid of saying the wrong thing.

I was afraid of doing the wrong thing.

THE PRESSURE OF FIELDING A GROUND BALL
COULD CAUSE RICKY TO FAINT.

I was so afraid it had even affected my physical appearance.

YEARS OF FEAR HAD RESULTED IN RICKY'S HAIR STANDING ON END PERMANENTLY.

The world was a scary place.

Scary thing number 10: Bullies

Scary thing number 9: Back hair

Scary thing number 8: Mold on the bread of your half-eaten peanut butter and jelly sandwich

Scary thing number 7: Clowns

Scary thing number 6: Bullies

Scary thing number 5: A dead bug in your drink

Scary thing number 4: Authority figures

Scary thing number 3: Pop quizzes

Scary thing number 2: Bullies (see pp. 6–7)

BOBBY SLOSH. A BULLY
WHO TOOK RICKY'S RATTLE
WHEN THEY WERE BOTH
BABIES.

BULLY OLIVER THURSTON BARNES
HAD EATEN RICKY'S LUNCH ALL
THROUGH FIRST GRADE.

RICKY'S THIRD GRADE BULLY WAS
VIN CRACKLE. VIN'S SPECIALTY
WAS REMOVING RICKY'S CAP AND
PLAYING KEEP-AWAY.

Scary thing number 1:

My life.

Which you'll read about in more detail
from here on in.

7

I was playing the most popular video game of
the summer: "Kill! Kill! Kill!"
My friend had destroyed most of my army.
All I had left was a wizard, three trolls, and eleven
village idiots.
Some friend.
His name: Fred Bologna.

FRED BOLOGNA

8

Although Fred Bologna had the tiniest eyes I had ever
seen when he took his glasses off, and although he was
an awful listener, he was my eyes and ears in a
neighborhood that was pretty much brand new to me.

I had lived here long, long ago.

The company my dad works for, Blatzfield's Foods, was now
moving back to their old headquarters.

This is the place where I saw my first lightning bug, toasted
my first marshmallow, and first laid eyes on the most
wonderful girl in the world, Sara Giacomo.

A lot had happened since I left, and Fred had been filling me
in on it.

Fred is my best friend in this town.

Not counting my grandma.

Thank goodness for her.

YAP
YAP

FRED WITHOUT GLASSES

9

Fred Bologna never uttered a word while playing a
  video game until he was sure he had the game well
  in hand. Once he did start speaking, neither he nor his
  army of annihilation could be stopped.
Fred took another of my village idiots.
This apparently spelled my doom, because the floodgates
  opened.
Fred spoke.

10

"I had the strangest dream last night. Very. Strange.
I mean. A big giant purple slimy kind of octopus was like
all over my living room, and my dad, he was just sleeping
on the couch. Snoring. Loudly. Like in real life. And this
big ol' octopus thing grabbed me, and its tentacles were all
oozing and mucusy and I was screaming, 'Help, Dad, a huge
giant oozing, mucusy, octopus thingy is about to devour
me whole!' and my dad just slept. And snored. Just like in
real life. And just as the huge octopus was about to put me
in his hideous jaws of death, I woke up. Imagine I didn't?
Wake up, I mean. I'd be dead right now. That's true, ya
know. If you die in your dream, you die in actual life. That's
a fact. I saw that on TV or something. And also read it in a
book. Plus it actually happened to my friend's cousin's
dentist's stepsister."

Fred had one of his elves, disguised as a knight, magic-
potion my three trolls to kingdom come.

"Also," Fred continued, "did you know a man in Ireland
lived for three years on nothing but toilet water? He got
trapped in his bathroom or something and he was stuck in
there for three years. Maybe four, I can't exactly recall.
Even worse was that he only had one magazine in there
with him. One. Could you imagine that? And it wasn't like
Video Gamer or something. That would be decent. But
here's the kicker: It was *Lady's Home Magazine*. I'd kill
myself. I'd get in the toilet and flush myself into oblivion, I
would. *Lady's Home Magazine!* Could you imagine? For
three years he had to read the same recipe for Meat Loaf
and Lima Bean Dip or some stuff like that. That's torture,
my friend."

Two more of my village idiots were wiped out. The victims
of a garden gnome's magic rake.

"**I**f I was a secret agent and an enemy spy put me on one of those torture racks, I wouldn't tell them a single secret. But if he said they were gonna lock me in a bathroom for three years with a copy of *Lady's Home Magazine*, I'd tell them everything. I'd crack. I couldn't take it. Gosh. Imagine taking the 'Are You and Your Spouse Compatible' quiz over and over and over again. How many times can a guy read '101 Holiday Decorations to Make with Felt.' I'd turn in my own dog. What a nightmare!"

In a bold move, three of my village idiots stormed the castle. My strategy was that Fred's wizards would be so surprised, they would not be able to react. This was not the case.

Poof, poof, and poof. My guys were turned into toads.

Boy, were my village idiots idiotic.

YAP
YAP

FRED BOLOGNA'S DOG

13

THREE OF FRED BOLOGNA'S FAVORITE ODORS

"**H**ow did he do it?" Fred asked. He didn't expect an answer, but just as I was trying to think of one anyway, he changed the subject. "Speaking of nightmares, we start sixth grade tomorrow. That's gotta stink.
Really bad.
Like poop, perhaps."

An anvil dropped on my wizard's head. He never had a chance.

Fred was unstoppable. "Speaking of poop, the summer is over. But we're starting sixth grade. Wow. I hear Keanu Dungston is a mean son of a so and so. He's been left back seven times. He runs that school. The first day of school, he gives as many wedgies to sixth graders as humanly possible. And not just your regular standard wedgie. He lifts your underwear out the back and up over your head."

My remaining village idiots were no longer under my control. In a panic they ran into each other over and over again until they knocked each other unconscious.

KEANU DUNGSTON

15

PRINCIPAL GIZZARD

"The worst thing is that Principal Gizzard is blind as a bat. Can't see a thing. So he doesn't see all the hideous evil that Dungston and his gang are showering on unsuspecting sixth graders. I heard that Dungston once superwedgied twelve sixth graders right in front of Principal Gizzard, and all that happened was the sixth graders got detention for crying in the halls. That's what you call blind justice, buddy. Face it: Our fellow sixth graders are doomed, my friend. They'd better say *adiós* to the carefree days of elementary school. I can't think of anything worse than the week they're about to face. Except maybe being locked in a bathroom with one issue of *Lady's Home Magazine*. It's a toss-up, I guess."

Fred's wizards captured my unconscious village idiots, but not until pointing and laughing at them for several minutes. Game over.

And based on what Fred had been saying, so was my life.

16

"But Fred, aren't you afraid of this Keanu guy?" I asked.

"Nope," he said.

"But why?"

"I don't smell."

"Smell?"

"Keanu can smell fear. If you are afraid, he will latch on to
your scent, hunt you down, and superwedgie you. I myself
am immune to fear. I'm blessed that way. You?"

Yikes.

I was covered in fear.

I was drenched in fear.

I was a factory of fear.

Yikes.

"Plus, his dad works for my mom, and Keanu's dad has strict
rules for his son about beating up the boss's kid. That
helps," added Fred.

The first day of school came quicker than I ever imagined.

RICKY SMOOTZ'S MOM

"Look at him, Father! Going into middle school for the first time today. Dressed all in his new middle school clothes. About to eat his new middle school breakfast. Good golly. I can still remember when he was getting diaper rash pimples and burping up cottage cheese-like substances that reeked to high heaven!" crooned my mom while serving up a two-foot stack of Blatzfield's New Improved, Half the Calorie, Frozen Chocolate Chip Cinnamon French Toast.

"Look at our boy all dressed up for his first day of middle school!" my mom shouted.

"I'm think of adding a third bathroom to our abode," said Dad.

"Lovely, dear. Simply lovely," singsonged Mom.

I rolled my eyes. I didn't mean to. But I did.

"Did you just roll your eyes, young man?" asked Dad.

YES seemed like a bad answer. NO would be a lie.

SEVEN TIES FOR A FIVE-DAY WORK WEEK OR THREE BATHROOMS FOR ONLY THREE PEOPLE. RICKY COULDN'T DECIDE WHICH WAS MORE PREPOSTEROUS.

I froze.

"Did you hear me, young man?"

I actually didn't hear that question because I was thinking about my answer to his first question.

"Are you trying to annoy me on purpose?" Dad asked.

"Yes," I said.

I was answering his initial question.

My father began to turn a tad red.

"If this is going to be an argument, I'm going upstairs," chimed in Mom.

And she did.

"Don't roll your eyes about bathrooms, if that's what you're rolling your eyes about!"

I swear I had to use every bit of strength not to roll my eyes.

"Better hygiene is what separates us from the finches and the pigs and the mammals! Better hygiene!" Dad told me.

The guy was kind of a neat freak.

"We *are* mammals, Dad," I said.

A loud screech from upstairs stopped the conversation before Dad could say, "I knew that."

RICKY SMOOTZ'S DAD

18

"**W**hat, heaven help us, is this!" yipped Mom, careening down the stairs, right arm fully extended in front of her, dangling the pair of underpants she had laid out for me the night before.

THE UNDERPANTS IN QUESTION

"My underwear," I correctly answered.

"Your bottom is briefless?" bristled my befuddled dad, barely able to breathe.

I was wearing pants, just no undies.

He went on.

"No briefs! What is the meaning of this? Have you no shame? That is inhuman! Intolerable! Disgusting! Immoral! That's what it is; immoral and unhygienic both! Get on some briefs and then get to that school of yours and learn how to be civilized!"

Parents. Wow.

19

I figured that if I went to school without underwear I would render myself wedgie-proof.

But my plans to foil Keanu Dungston's great wedgie free-for-all had gone the way of the dodo.

I was forced to underize.

The first day of sixth grade was pretty much the worst day of my life.

And I hadn't even left the house yet.

I needed a new plan. But what?

RICKY THINKING

When I got on the bus, I was greeted by
Constance.

She was huge.

Her smile was huger.

She was apparently the happiest woman in the world.

Or completely off her rocker.

Only time would tell.

"Welcome aboard, sonny; next stop – the deepest, darkest
dimensions of humankind!" she said.

Oh boy.

"Just kidding," Constance added.

Thank goodness, I thought.

"One more stop and then the deepest, darkest dimensions
of humankind!" exclaimed Constance, again. And for
good measure, she laughed wildly.

Off her rocker, it was.

CONSTANCE

I sat in the first seat available.

I had heard that for a sixth grader to enter the back
quarter of a middle school bus would be suicide.

The eighth graders were back there.

And not just any eighth graders.

These guys were apparently so mean, the only thing they had
to offer the rest of the world was a sock in the arm.

Or worse.

That's who was back there.

THE BOYS IN THE BACK OF THE BUS

RICKY

22

The stress was getting to me.

I was spent.

I closed my eyes.

Just for what felt like a second. But it wasn't a second.

Because Constance the bus driver's tonsils were
waggling before my eyes.

She was right up in my face.

Yelling, but smiling, too.

"We're here, sleeping beauty! Wake up and smell the
pizza-bagels!"

"Huh?" I asked in a groggy voice.

"Get off my bus, you little bugger – the torture
chamber awaits!"

A HOT DOG THAT'S BEEN COOKING ON ONE OF THOSE
ROLLING MACHINES FOR 17 YEARS IN THE CAFETERIA OF
RICHARD M. NIXON MIDDLE SCHOOL.

As I stepped off the bus and took in the magnificent
architectural splendor that was Richard M. Nixon Middle
School I thought:

Hey self,

this

can't

be

all

that

bad.

I watched the kids talking and joking with one another under
majestic oak trees that made the place look like an
enchanted forest.

None of these kids seemed worried.

Sara Giacomo, the girl I'd had a crush on since I last lived here
but had never actually made eye contact with, waved to me.

SARA GIACOMO.
RICKY SMOOTZ'S
DREAM DATE.

Things were going to be all right.

Thwart!

Goopht!

Zing!

Swoosh!

Everything went black, and for a fleeting moment I thought I
   had dropped dead.

But it was more awful than that.

I had been superwedgied in plain sight of practically every kid
   in town.

"Welcome to Richard M. Nixon Middle School!" said a
   completely oblivious Principal Gizzard.

When I got my head out from my underwear I witnessed some
   of the most unpleasant sights imaginable.

I saw Sara Giacomo running by me screaming in the most
   high-pitched tone I had ever heard.

That is, until a millisecond later when I saw Fred running by
   screaming in an even higher pitch.

Then I saw the face of pure evil emerging from behind a bush.

"You've been Keanued!" it snarled.

I certainly had.

I certainly had.

First period. Science. Mrs. Vandeguarde.

"Hello class, I'm Mrs. Vandeguarde."

She wrote it on the blackboard.

"I'm firm, but fair."

She had blue hair.

"I always loved science. Even when I was little."

I raised my hand.

"Yes, boy who was superwedgied earlier today?"

"Me?" I asked.

"Yes, you."

"Did your hair turn blue in an experiment gone haywire?"

I didn't really say that.

I can't even raise my hand to ask to go to the bathroom.

I'm afraid of public speaking.

Sheesh, I'm afraid of public just-sitting-there.

25

I had five minutes in between first and second period. I
    figured that gave me forty-five seconds for a phone call.
I needed to call Grandma to settle my nerves.
My grandma is sometimes the only person I can talk to.
My grandma is my hero.
"Grandma, I got trouble."
"What?"
"Bully."
"Bully?"
"Yep, a bully."
"I got two words
    for you."
"What?"

RICKY SMOOTZ'S GRANDMA

"Crazy Enzio."
"That cowboy you used to tell me about?"
"The very one. Your great-grandfather's second cousin's
    grandmother's brother."
"I'm too old for that stuff to work on me now."
"I got three words for you then."
"What?"
"I love you."
"Oh, Grandma."
"You're not too old for that stuff are you?"
"Kinda."
I wasn't at all.

Second period. Math. Ms. Brazil.

"Ms. Brazil, kids! That's me. Three cheers for me."
We all just sat there.
By the way, Ms. Brazil was all nostrils.
"I'm your pre-algebra teacher!" she said proudly.
She high-fived Fred.
Yep, Fred was in my math class.
Sitting in the front row.
I was seated behind him.
"I think numbers can be

FUN, FUN, FUN, FUN, FUN, FUN!" she cheered.
I wrote YIKES, YIKES, YIKES, YIKES, YIKES, YIKES on a
  piece of paper and handed it to Fred.
Naturally, he read it aloud.
She sent Fred to the principal's office.
The fun was apparently over.

27

Third period. English. Mr. Flappy.

"I am Flappy. Mr. Flappy."

Mr. Flappy seemed like a nice guy.

He had only one giant hairy eyebrow. A unibrow. Frankly, it
should have been on my top scariest things list.

I really didn't want to be rude, but it was hard not to stare.

"I like words," he announced.

He opened a dictionary.

Held one hand over his eyes.

Pointed to a word in the book with the other hand.

Uncovered his eyes.

Looked down.

Read the word aloud.

"Platitude."

He seemed happy with himself.

"Say it with me. Platitude. Say it. Platitude."

MR. FLAPPY'S EYEBROW. OR IS IT A
CATIPILLAR?

We wouldn't.

"Platttttitudddde. It is beautiful. Say it with me,
Platttttitudddde."

We said it this time.

"You, over there!" said Mr. Flappy, looking directly at me.

"Me?"

"Yes, the boy who was totally humiliated in front of the entire
school this morning. Come up here and point to a word at
random."

I did.

"Now read it to the class."

I paused for what seemed like an hour.

"Effervescence," I finally said.

That filled Mr. Flappy with joy.

"What a beautiful word. Say it with me, class. Effervescence.
Effffffffferrrrvvvessssssssssennnnnnnce."

The word I'd really pointed to was "caterpillar."

Yikes.

That's exactly what his eyebrow looked like! A giant caterpillar!
There was no way I was saying that.

Fourth period. Lunch. With a peanut butter and jelly
  sandwich and Fred Bologna.
Interestingly enough, Bologna was eating ham.

"I never knew you were that stinky," Fred said.
I just kept looking around to see if Keanu had the same lunch
  period as us.
Fred continued.
"The smell of your fear must be powerful stuff. Boy, oh boy.
  And you're gonna get that every day unless you de-stink
  yourself." Fred stared at me. I stared at Fred. "How?" I
  asked. "You gotta become like that cowboy your grandma
  used to tell you stories about. What was the name of that
  dude? Kooky Bill?"
"Crazy Enzio."
"Oh yeah, Crazy Enzio! He was cool. Didn't he tame grizzly
  bears by playing the kazoo?"
"Harmonica."

"And instead of guns didn't he carry peanut butter and jelly sandwiches in his holsters?"

"Loaves of Italian bread."

"And didn't he invent time zones so he could be in California to stop a bank robbery and in New Jersey for a pajama party, which were both scheduled to take place at seven o'clock?"

"Not a pajama party, his wedding."

"I love Kooky Bill!"

"Crazy Enzio."

"Yeah, Crazy Enzio. Your aunt is the best."

"My grandma!"

"That was a joke. Of course I know your grandma. She's the best."

CRAZY ENZIO

29

F ifth period. Art class. Mrs. Link. She seemed
very nice.

Sixth period. Gym. Mr. Blunkard. Very uncoordinated. Thin
as a toothpick. Incredibly thick glasses. The first gym
teacher I ever truly liked.

Seventh period was history. And after history the first day of
school was history as well.

Yahoo.

30

Fred and I played video games after school.

He said, "Blah blah blah blah blah blah blah blah blah blah blah blah blah blah blah blah blah blah blah blah blah blah blah blah blah blah blah blah blah blah blah blah blah blah blah blah blah blah blah blah blah blah blah blah blah blah blah blah blah blah blah blah blah blah blah blah blah blah blah blah blah blah blah blah blah blah blah blah blah blah blah blah blah blah blah blah blah blah blah blah blah blah blah blah!"

"Blah blah blah blah blah blah blah blah

blah blah blah blah blah blah blah blah

blah blah blah blah blah blah blah blah

blah blah blah blah blah blah blah blah

blah blah blah blah blah blah blah blah

blah blah blah blah blah blah blah blah

blah blah blah blah blah blah blah blah

blah blah blah blah blah blah blah blah

blah blah blah blah blah blah blah blah

blah blah blah blah blah blah blah blah

blah blah?"

32

"Blah blah blah blah blah blah blah blah blah

blah blah blah blah blah blah blah blah blah

blah blah blah blah blah blah blah blah blah

blah blah blah blah blah blah blah blah blah

blah blah blah blah blah blah blah blah blah

blah blah blah blah blah blah blah blah blah

blah blah blah blah blah blah blah blah blah

blah blah blah blah blah blah blah blah blah!"

33

That might not be exactly what Fred said.

But it was exactly what I heard.

And I wasn't seeing too well, either.

Because I swear all his men were Keanu Dungstons.

And that they were superwedgieing each and every one
  of my elves, knights, wizards, and ogres.

I had to get out of there.

Fast.

"Fred," I said. "I have to get out of here. Fast."

He said, "Blah blah blah."

"Okay, I'll see you tomorrow."

"Blah blah!"

"Bye."

34

That night I had a dream about sharing a milk shake
   with Sara Giacomo.

I guess that literally made her the girl of my dreams.

It was like we were in a movie.

It was kind of sweet.

Until she turned into Keanu Dungston and superwedgied me.

Needless to say, I had a pretty restless night.

And I must've sleepwalked at some point, because when I
   looked in the mirror that morning I was wearing my
   cowboy hat and neckerchief.

And I swear my reflection spoke to me.

"I'm ready when you are," it said.

My, my.

I certainly was losing it.

Mom said as she served up a plate of Blatzfield's Jumbo-Sized, Just Add Water and Stir, Instant, Now Fortified with Calcium, Scrambled Eggs: "I've found some of the most heart-tugging home movies of you, honey-pooh. There's even one moment where you're hugging your Baby-Wet-My-Pants dolly. There you are, unabashedly expressing your feelings for Baby-Wet-My-Pants, for the world to see. And see it they will!" she sang. "NO ONE and I repeat NO ONE sees that footage!" I yelped. "Just for that outburst, young man, I will personally see to it that you and Baby-Wet-My-Pants are played on a continual loop on our living room TV for every guest's amusement!" said Dad.

"I think that is a dandy idea . . . Ricky: The Diaper Years,"
  chimed in Mom as though she were announcing the year's
  Academy Award® winner for Best Picture.
"Honey bunny, I was trying to teach the boy a lesson," said
  Dad. "For his own good."
"I'm sure people would love seeing my little suggie woogie
  suggie woogie suggie!"
I don't think I'm exaggerating all that much, my mom really
  talks like that.

My parents or Keanu Dungston.
Dungston or my parents.
It was a tough choice.
But choices like that were out of my hands.
It was time to catch the bus.

RICKY WAS SURE HE SHRUNK WHEN-
EVER HIS MOM SPOKE ALL LOVEY-
DOVEY, COSTING HIM A CAREER
AS A PRO BASKETBALL STAR.

On the bus I fell asleep again.

My body was tired, but my mind was still going a million miles
a minute.

I had another dream.

Looking down from way above the land I saw a giant
gathering of kids.

They were carrying another kid on their shoulders.

As I got closer I saw that they were the kids from
my school.

And the kid they were carrying was me.

I dreamed that the whole school was shouting my name.

"Smootz!

  Smootz!

  Smootz!

  Smootz!"

It was great.

Then I heard,

  "SMMMMMMMMOOOOOOOOTZZZZZZZZ!"

It was Constance.

We had reached Richard M. Nixon Middle School.

Too bad.

But something was different.

I walked off that bus filled with a crazy beautiful confidence.

37

DUNGSTON'S GANG

And as fate would have it, the first thing I saw when
I entered school that day was the face of my tormentor,
Keanu Dungston. But I was ready.

"A-hem," I said as I tippy-toed over to Dungston and three of
his henchmen.

When they ignored me, I repeated the "A-hem" and added
"Mr. D-D-D-Dungston?"

Keanu got right up in my face and said, "Are you talkin' to me?"

I swear I nearly died right there from his world-record bad
breath.

His gang giggled like a bunch of weasels at a pajama party.

"Take care of him, boys," ordered Keanu.

Next thing I knew I was superwedgied. Again.

Pitiful.

That's when I realized this was not something I could do alone.
I needed help. Big-time.

What I didn't realize was what a truly awful day I was in for.

44

38

In first period science, Mrs. Vandeguarde was
   pummeled with a barrage of spitballs. It was like a great
   fireworks display.
The colored construction paper spitballs were majestic
   spheres of yellow and red and orange.
They bounced off the incredible blue of Mrs. Vandeguarde's
   hair and drew gasps of awe from the kids in class.
There was even a big finale that was timed perfectly to a
   nicely performed kazoo rendition of "The Star-Spangled
   Banner."
As the last spitball hit pay dirt, the spectators launched into
   a spontaneous standing ovation that lasted fifteen
   minutes.
Then everything went quiet.
All eyes turned to me.

MRS. VANDEGUARDE'S SPLATTERED EYEWEAR

On my desk was a pile of colored construction paper
    spitballs, a kazoo, and the smoking gun that said
    "guilty beyond a reasonable doubt": a dripping straw.
I looked around the room. I got a quick glimpse of Keanu
    Dungston pointing and laughing through the narrow
    window on the door to Mrs. Vandeguarde's classroom.
I was set up.
Framed.
Bamboozled.
I somehow made it through the rest of the day.
There was only one thing left for me to do.
I would never return to Richard M. Nixon Middle School.
Ever.

Have you ever played sick?

Some kids are just terrible at it.

They gasp.

They moan.

They pathetically whisper every word as if it were their last.

This leaves their parents two choices:

A) Call the undertaker.

B) Call the Bad Acting police.

Even if it works, overdoing
    is a big, big mistake. When
    you pretend to be that
    sick, you're thrown in
    bed, forced to take awful-
    tasting medicine, and
    prohibited from
    participating in any
    worthwhile activity.

Would you like to know the
  foolproof method for playing sick?
It's really quite simple.
Just say you're nauseous.
Right off the bat, you've unnerved your victim.
Nobody wants to be puked on.
And there's no way to prove if you're nauseous or not — it's
  your word against your elder's better judgment.
And since everyone knows nausea comes and goes, when
  your complete recovery coincides with your friends
  getting home from school, it won't seem so conveniently
  unbelievable.
Perfect, isn't it?

40

"You used the nauseous ploy, didn't you?" my grandma gently scolded.

I had just been deposited at her house for sick care.

"I was desperate, Grandma. Besides, you're the one who taught it to me," I said.

"Yes, but I said to only use it in extreme emergencies."

"Well, this is the extremist. It's Keanu Dungston. He's a dirty, rotten, smelly, evil, disgusting, worthless, unprecious—"

"I bet he was precious when he was born."

"Well he's not now, I'll tell you that."

"Maybe you're not trying hard enough to see the good in him."

I launched into the whole Keanu Dungston saga from the indoctrinating wedgie to the star-bangled catastrophe. "He just needs someone to set him straight is all," said Grandma.

"Yeah, but who?"

"You."

"Me?"

"No, the man on the moon. Of course, you!"

She gave me one of her patented hugs and for a moment, all my troubles

ATTILA THE HUN COULD'VE USED A HUG FROM RICKY'S GRANDMA.

seemed to be absorbed by her ample body. If all the world leaders could get a hug from my grandma each day, there would never be another war.

41

"Tell me a Crazy Enzio story?" I asked.

"Really?"

"Yes really, Grandma."

"Did I ever tell you the one about Crazy Enzio coming face-to-face with his first rattlesnake?"

"Never. Tell me. Please."

42

"**O**ne moonlit night, way out on the open prairie, while cooking a pot of minestrone soup over the open fire, Crazy Enzio took notice of an approaching rattlesnake. That might sound frightening enough to you, but what you don't know is that way back in those days, rattlesnakes were huge – an average rattlesnake was big enough to have 4,230,000,000,000,000,001 Western-style boots made out of him. A rattler's fangs alone were pretty near the size of the Empire State Building in New York City. And this one was very perturbed and just one hundred feet away!

"Enzio calmly took out his harmonica Bernadine and began playing. Bernadine had never failed to soothe even the most savage of savage beasts, but since the rattlesnake didn't have ears, it wasn't very effective and the crazed giant kept slithering toward Enzio. At this point, most men would've grabbed a pen and some paper and started writing out their last will and testament. But not Crazy Enzio.

"When the snake was twenty-five feet away and closing fast, it occurred to Enzio . . . IF I DON'T BOTHER IT, IT WON'T BOTHER ME. But a fraction of a second later he was swooped up by a stupendous tongue. As he was being squeezed of all life, he remembered . . . THAT ONLY WORKS WITH BEES. Most people would have thrown in the towel. But not Crazy Enzio.

"The tongue retracted back into the snake's mouth, dragging Crazy Enzio in with it. Enzio rolled into a ball, figuring as long as he was swallowed whole, he would be free when the snake had its next bowel movement. What Enzio didn't realize was snakes of the Old West loved chewing, and in seconds he was bit into tiny pieces. But did Crazy Enzio give up. No!

"His arms, feet, and elbows started to meet in the lower intestines of the snake. His quick-thinking head knew there was still time to reattach the parts, so the head painstakingly rolled them all in the anatomically correct place. But just as his left foot was being positioned, the snake let out a monstrous belch and Crazy Enzio's parts went every which way. Now, not even all the king's horses and all the king's men could put him back together again.

"Crazy Enzio was a goner. But was
that going to stop him? No way!
The story goes he met God at
the Gates of Heaven and the
two became great friends right
off the bat. One night in a card
game, Crazy Enzio wagered his
cowboy hat against being put back
on Earth two minutes before the
snake ate him. God said okay to
that and raised him by promising
to make snakes smaller and non-
chewers against Enzio's harmonica,
Bernadine. Crazy Enzio agreed
and showed God that he had two
pairs — aces over threes. God

CRAZY ENZIO IN
HEAVEN

revealed that all he had was jack high. So Crazy Enzio
was put back on Earth two minutes before he was to be
a rattler's dinner. This time when the tiny snake
approached, Enzio ran like heck. *You can't be too
careful*, was his thinking.
"The End."

"That was great. I love that!" I screamed.

I hugged Grandma.

44

"What am I going to do about Keanu?" I asked.

"Maybe you need some help." Grandma replied.

"That's exactly what I think. Like some really big moosey guys."

"Haven't you learned anything from Crazy Enzio?"

"Hmm."

"He uses brain, not brawn."

"My brain doesn't work so well lately."

"That's because it's filled with fear."

"I'm afraid you're right."

"And what I meant by some help is you need to do something to bring out the part of you that isn't afraid."

"What?"

"Only then will you think straight enough to outsmart Keanu."

"Huh?"

"Only then will you have the courage to pull off your plan."

"I'm not following."

"You will. Only now we have a funeral to attend."

45

This was no ordinary funeral. But then, my grandma was no ordinary grandmother. She led me into her bathroom. "Annie and Jimmy, two of my favorite cockroaches, met their demise," said Grandma.

"That's so saaaaaaaddddd," I said, not even knowing myself if I was serious or not.

A N N I E

"Too much TV is what killed them." I just sat there openmouthed, dumbfounded, in total awe of my grandma and her incredible world.

"Yes, I was carrying that twenty-one-inch set from the living room to my bedroom and it was heavy, so I put it on the floor for a minute while I caught my breath and when I lifted it up again there were Jimmy and Annie, flat as fettuccini. It was too much TV for them. If I had only had a thirteen-inch set, they might still be alive today. Let that be a lesson. Too much TV is really, really bad for you."

JIMMY

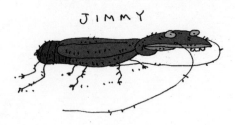

46

In a touching ceremony, Grandma flushed Annie and
  Jimmy into their next life.
Before she sent them off she spoke about them beautifully.
Annie, apparently, was a special cockroach, who loved
  pumpkin butter, being read to on rainy nights, and
  home runs in the bottom of the ninth.
Jimmy also was special. He, ironically, loved TV, but he also
  lived for the moment and was up for every challenge life
  had to offer.

THE KILLER

47

A funny thing happened as I watched Jimmy swirl
around the bowl. Jimmy went round and round and round,
and I went into a kind of trance.

I saw myself in my cowboy getup.

I remembered how wearing that stuff made me feel smarter,
braver, special, impressive.

Suddenly everything Grandma was saying made perfect sense.

That's whose help I needed.

That kid in the cowboy suit.

Much to my surprise, these words came out of my mouth:

> THERE'S GONNA BE A SHOWDOWN AT THE O.K. CORRAL! SO TIE UP YOUR DOGGIES, PUT YOUR KIDS TO BED, AND HOLD ON TO YOUR BONNET! COWBOY BOY IS ABOUT TO RIDE INTO THIS ONE-HORSE TOWN!

"Shhhhhhhhh!" shot back Grandma. "Can't you see I'm about
to finish up a funeral here?"

Mom picked me up at 5:15 P.M.

I had miraculously been cured of all my ills.

"I've found the most adorable pictures of you and all your
    neighborhood friends. You're older than you were in the
    video stuff, but you still have Baby-Wet-My-Pants. Isn't that
    the sweetest?" sang my mom as she handed me the 9 x 12
    manila envelope stuffed with photos.

Now I felt nauseous.

THE MANILA ENVELOPE
OF HORRORS

"**W**ell, if it isn't my sweet little cowboy boy,"
   shrilled my mom.

I had just come down for breakfast dressed in my
   cowboy suit.

I had on a huge Western hat.

A neckerchief.

Boots.

A vest.

And unusually fuzzy pants.

THE HUGE HAT

The outfit had always been too big for me and now it fit
   perfectly.

I was spectacular.

THE
NECKERCHIEF

THE BOOTS

THE VEST

THE UNUSUALLY
FUZZY PANTS

"You going to school like that?" asked my dad.

"I reckon," I said with a bit of a twang.

"The boy's gone bonkers!" Dad exclaimed.

"Good woman, could you rustle me up some grub. I gotta rid
  the school of a wily varmint today and I need my strength,"
  I said to Mom.

"Bet a Blatzfield's Triple Chocolate Swirled Frosted
  Raspberry Filled All Imitation Pastry Nutrasweetened
  Toaster Tart would do the trick," sang my mom.

"Yup," I replied, "I reckon it would."

50

When I got on the bus that morning, Constance the
bus driver with the elastic smile greeted me loudly, "Holy
Cow Droppings, what the heck is that getup?"

"Ma'am, did anyone ever tell you that your smile could light up
a campfire in a rainstorm?"

"Oh, go on," Constance giggled daintily.

I walked straight to the rear of the bus.

All the backseat bullies sat up at attention.

They were waiting like spiders for a fly to enter their web.

"I reckon you boys won't mind if I take this here empty seat."

An especially large member of the group spoke up.

"If you sit there, me and the boys are gonna scramble your
brains into a Western omelet."

I sat in the seat just the same.

I was no longer afraid because with my new way of thinking
I had come up with a breakthrough theory about
these guys.

Just as the ignoramuses were about to pounce on me, I
deployed my new strategy.

"Big Poopy Diapers!" I yelled.

51

RICKY WOULD HAVE GONE FOR THE ARMPIT FART BUT HE THOUGHT THAT MIGHT BE TOO SOPHISTICATED FOR HIS AUDIENCE.

I followed that up with:

"Royal *Flush!*"

Cleverly emphasizing the word "flush."

Comedy 101

1. PLACE HAND FLATLY UNDER ARM PIT.

2. FLAP OTHER ARM UP & DOWN LIKE CRAZED CHICKEN.

And I finished it off with this brilliant poem:

"Gene, Gene. Made a machine.

Frank, Frank. Turned the crank.

Art, Art. Made a fart.

And blew the whole darn thing apart."

FRANK, FRANK ATTEMPTING
TO TURN THE CRANK

The delinquents went wild with laughter.

You see, I now knew that guys like the
    ones who surrounded me found
        humor having to do with biological functions
        completely irresistible.

53

The back-of-the-bus boys all gathered around, continually high-fiving me – the male-bonding ritual that means you have been accepted into the pack.

From then on, the goof-offs held me in high regard.

I, likewise, learned that they weren't such bad guys after all.

I discovered that they had feelings like normal people and, at the very worst, they were just big, misguided lugs.

My guess is while a few of them would go on to become career criminals, maybe one of them, thanks to my encouragement, would grow up to be a success – perhaps a doctor specializing in gastrology.

The first thing I did when I got to Richard M. Nixon Middle School was to swagger directly to the office of Principal Gizzard.

"Sir, there's a bad guy in these parts who's been perpetratin' the most heinous of crimes upon the cowpokes of our fair school. He must be taken down. And I'm the fella who can do it," I announced.

"I see," replied the both near- and far-sighted Principal Gizzard.

I continued. "Since you run this town, I just wanted your permission to take this dastardly coyote (which I pronounced *kie-oat*) in."

"My permission?"

"Not for nothing, pardner, but Ricky Smootz always gets his man and/or adolescent male."

"Ricky Smootz! *You're* Ricky Smootz?"

"Known in some parts as Cowboy Boy."

"You're the guy who unmercifully sprayed a teacher with moist wads of paper to the tune of this great nation's theme song!"

"I was framed," I drawled.

"You have detention, buster. You are spending the entire day in the corner of my office writing "The Star-Spangled Banner" over and over. And then, I want you to tear the pages you've written into 100,000,000,000 moist wads of paper. And then, I want you to do something I haven't thought of yet but will decide on after I consult the best punishers in the school!"

"Dag nabbit," I muttered under my breath.

I took his undeserved punishment like all real cowboys do – with quiet reserve.

Occasionally I took out my harmonica, which I'd named Loretta, to play an around-the-campfire sort of tune.

The world would have to wait one more day to be saved from Keanu Dungston.

RICKY BELTS OUT A POLKA-
STYLE COWBOY DITTY.

55

Played "Kill Kill Kill!" with Fred Bologna after
 school.
We didn't say much.

Because Fred was losing badly.
I had on my Cowboy Boy clothes, after all.

56

On the day you're about to read about, many amazing things happened.

The president signed a law making it illegal for a teacher to continually say at the end of the year, "You are the best class I ever had," no matter how awful that year's class had been.

In Ohio, a group of deer went up to a hunter, tweaked his nose, turned his hat around, and robbed him of fifty-seven cents and a pack of Juicy Fruit gum.

The boy with the world's largest collection of video games turned off his system, trashed his entire collection, and went outside to play.

While destroying an entire population of cretin aliens for the one zillionth time, it suddenly occurred to him that it had become boring three years ago.

But nothing was more astounding than the events that took place in a five-minute time period, in one hallway, at Richard M. Nixon Middle School.

The halls were empty. Everyone was in homeroom
except me, a.k.a. Cowboy Boy, and Keanu Dungston, the
perennial eighth grader.

I was standing at one end of the hall.

Keanu Dungston stood at the other.

I was wearing the hat, the neckerchief, the vest, the fuzzy
pants, the whole ball o' wax.

Keanu was wearing the demonic smirk he always wore.

And a black hat.

The bad guys always wore a black hat.

This hat just happened to be of the baseball variety.

BALL O' WAX

"**H**owdy, Dungston!" I hollered.

Dungston looked up.

I pounded my chest.

"You're a wanted man and I'm taking you in, Dungston."

But Keanu Dungston didn't hear me.

I assumed he was thinking about a joke someone had told him a few days ago that he didn't quite get.

"This school ain't big enough for the both of us, *hombre!*" I yelled again.

Dungston laughed.

He had probably finally figured out the joke.

It was time to get a new fence, because the big elephant broke it when he sat on it. Funny!

I'm sure that was going on in his thick skull.

WHAT TIME IS IT WHEN AN ELEPHANT SITS ON A FENCE?

"I'm taking you down, Dungston!" I bellowed.

Dungston's eyes got huge. He heard me this time.

I stared down Keanu.

Keanu stared back.

I squinted.

Keanu squinted.

I blinked one eye.

Keanu blinked one eye.

I stuck out my tongue.

Keanu stuck out his tongue.

I crossed my eyes and stuck out my tongue.

Keanu did likewise.

We both were masters of intimidation.

60

I decided to go for it all.

I rubbed my tummy while simultaneously patting the top of my head.

Keanu tried for a moment, but he couldn't handle the complex maneuver.

Round one went to me.

61

Sensing Keanu's confusion, I decided to bypass round two and go straight in for the win.

I reached into my vest for my "secret weapon."

Keanu laughed loudly. The big, big elephant broke the little tiny fence, he must have thought to himself.

"Change your ways, Dungston, or you're finished in this town," I said. "I got the goods on you."

Keanu's eyes focused on the 9 x 12 envelope I was waving over my head.

"Whatta you gonna do, fan me to death, you . . . you . . . Cowboy Boy!" yelled Keanu.

62

"**N**o, you dang varmint, I'm gonna show the world
   what's inside unless you turn over a new leaf," I
   screamed.

I pulled an 8 x 10 glossy out of the envelope.

It was a picture of a young Keanu Dungston.

A Keanu Dungston who just happened to be at a party held
   by my mom oh so many years ago.

And the interesting thing was that, back then, Keanu
   apparently had a sweet side.

There he was, in full color, hugging Baby-Wet-My-Pants
   with one arm and feeding her
   a ba-ba with the other.

Who would've thought that way
   back when, Keanu Dungston
   and I would share an affinity
   for Baby-Wet-My-Pants!

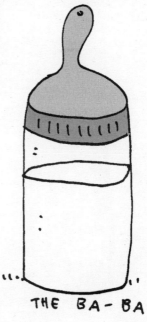

THE BA-BA

And right then, we both knew, once a picture like that got out,
    it would be hard for anyone to truly fear Dungston.
He would be humiliated, and his reign of terror would be over.
It was the perfect plan. A plan I'd concocted as soon as I'd put
    on my complete cowboy wardrobe.

63

But I was willing to give Dungston a way out.

"Stop bullying everyone!

Do one good deed for everyone you ever wedgied!

And brush after every meal!

If you do those three things, no one will ever see this

here picture."

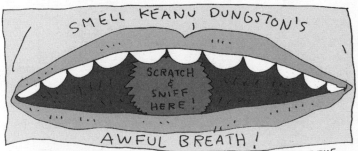

SMELL KEANU DUNGSTON'S

SCRATCH & SNIFF HERE!

AWFUL BREATH!

* IF NO SMELL IS RELEASED, YOU MUST LIVE IN ONE OF THE 38 STATES THAT HAVE OUTLAWED KEANU DUNGSTON'S BREATH.

64

A sense of relief seemed to pass through Keanu Dungston's evil body. He didn't have to be the bad guy anymore. He could actually share the love he felt for the rest of humanity. None of this had ever occurred to him before. You could actually see that he was filled with joy.

He skipped down the hall and gave me an embrace of friendship. Keanu would later tell people he felt like he was running in slow motion through a sun-drenched field of lilies.

I felt differently.

Horrified by the oncoming Dungston, I ducked just as I was about to be mauled.

Keanu sailed over me and into the lockers, knocking himself more senseless than usual.

The bell rang.

Homeroom was over.

Students poured into that hallway.

There, they saw me standing over a flat-on-his-back, disheveled Keanu Dungston.

Everyone was silent.

Dumbfounded.

Amazed by the sight.

Dungston lifted his banged-up head and said these now immortal words:

"This Cowboy Boy you see before you has taught me a very valuable lesson. I'm gonna be nice now!"

The crowd went crazy.

I was a hero.

And that was that.

DUNGSTON'S GANG FLED THE SCENE LIKE THE CHICKENS THEY WERE.

Fred and I hung out after school as usual.

"You are a hero. Capital 'H.' Capital 'ERO.' Which means I'm
your side kick. Every hero has a side kick. The Green
Hornet had Kato. The Lone Ranger had Tonto. Superman
had . . . well . . . Superman had no one. But he wasn't even a
human, so he doesn't count. You are gonna need a side kick.
Together we can make the world safe for niceness and
goodness and kick evil in its big fat jelly-butt. Kids all over
town are calling you Cowboy Boy. What should they call
me? I was thinking maybe Batboy Boy. Get it? I could speak
softly but carry a forty-two-ounce Louisville Slugger. I
wonder if they'll erect a statue of you? Of course, they
usually only erect statues of dead guys. . . ."

Fred went on and on.

I told him that I wouldn't even need the cowboy outfit anymore.
That I'd learned what I needed to learn about myself, and I
could now take on the world in everyday attire.

Fred whooped, "Kill! Kill! Kill!"

All I had left were two trolls, a knight, an ogre, and seven
village idiots.

This is not an excuse. But my mind was a million miles away.

I was proud of myself. I had faced my fears and beat them silly.

I was no longer Ricky V. Smootz.

I was more like Ricky N. Smootz.

The "N" is for Not Very Afraid.

IT COULD HAPPEN.

Then the phone rang.

Fred said it was for me.

He was right.

It was Sara Giacomo, the girl of my dreams previously mentioned on pages 10, 26, and 40.

"Ricky, you were wonderful."

"I was? Yes. I was."

"I have a problem. I need Cowboy Boy. Will you help?"

I was trembling. Yet I managed to get these words out of my mouth:

"I sure can, lil' missy. Cowboy Boy is ready and willin'."

"I love you, Ricky Smootz!"

Should I have told her I loved her back?

Should I have said something aloof?

Luckily, I didn't need to concern myself with any of that.

I had already passed out.

I'm probably going to need
the hat,
the vest,
the harmonica,
the neckerchief,
and the unusually fuzzy pants, after all.

Who knows, I may even need Batboy Boy.

Let's hope not.

The End.

FRED AS BATBOY BOY

About the Author

James Proimos, the author of this here book, is no cowboy. But he does dream of having a farm one day where he can feed his pony apples.

He currently lives in the quiet western town of Baltimore with his lovely wife, Jolie; his two cockroaches, Annie and Jimmy; and a gaggle of other critters.